P9-AGF-596

WHEN YOU WISH

UPON A STAR

Words by
Ned Washington
Illustrations by
Alexandra Day

THE GREEN TIGER PRESS
San Diego
1987

For my father.
-A.D.

"WHEN YOU WISH UPON A STAR", Words by Ned Washington,
    Music by Leigh Harline. Copyright © 1940 by
    Bourne Co. Copyright reserved. All rights reserved.
    Used by permission.
Illustrations copyright © 1987 by Alexandra Day.
The Green Tiger Press
First Edition • Second Printing
Library of Congress Catalog Card No. 86-83256
ISBN 0-88138-087-3

The paintings for this book were done in egg tempera.
The typeface is Della Robbia set by TypeLink of San Diego.
Color separations by Photolitho AG, Gossau-Zurich, Switzerland.
Printed and bound in Hong Kong.

Star light, star bright
First star I see tonight
I wish I may
I wish I might
Have the wish
I wish tonight.

MAKES
NO
DIFFERENCE
WHO YOU ARE

CITY POUND

...AS DREAMERS DO

The sweet fulfillment of

FATE STEPS IN AND SEES YOU THR- OUGH